START YOUR ENGINES!

LOWRIDERS

By Martha London

Kaleidoscope
Minneapolis, MN

The Quest for Discovery Never Ends

This edition first published in 2020 by Kaleidoscope Publishing, Inc.

No part of this publication may be reproduced in whole or in part without written permission of the publisher.

For information regarding permission, write to
Kaleidoscope Publishing, Inc.
6012 Blue Circle Drive
Minnetonka, MN 55343

Library of Congress Control Number
2019940180

ISBN
978-1-64519-058-5 (library bound)
978-1-64494-216-1 (paperback)
978-1-64519-159-9 (ebook)

Text copyright © 2020 by Kaleidoscope Publishing, Inc. All-Star Sports, Bigfoot Books, and associated logos are trademarks and/or registered trademarks of Kaleidoscope Publishing, Inc.

Printed in the United States of America.

FIND ME IF YOU CAN!

Bigfoot lurks within one of the images in this book. It's up to you to find him!

TABLE OF
CONTENTS

Chapter 1: Low and Slow **4**

Chapter 2: A Sense of Identity **10**

Chapter 3: Cruisin' **16**

Chapter 4: Center of Attention **22**

Beyond the Book 28
Research Ninja 29
Further Resources 30
Glossary 31
Index 32
Photo Credits 32
About the Author 32

CHAPTER 1

Low and Slow

The San Francisco sun was bright and warm. Roberto and his dad stood on the sidewalk behind a metal barrier. They weren't allowed on the street. The parade was about to start. Lots of people performed. But Roberto was there for the cars. Soon, lowriders drove down the street.

Lowrider parades are opportunities for drivers to show off their cars.

Cars of every color glinted in the sunlight. People took pictures in front of the lowriders. Loud music blasted from the car stereos. Roberto saw Chevys, Cadillacs, and Lincolns. All of them had **modifications**. The bumpers sat low to the ground. Roberto was sure the paint was going to scrape off. But it didn't.

Roberto craned his neck. He wanted to see inside the cars. Some of them had special **upholstery**. One red car had velvet fabric on the seats and the ceiling. Roberto and his dad didn't say anything. They wouldn't have been able to hear each other anyway. The cheering crowd and rumbling cars were too loud. But Roberto smiled up at his dad. His dad smiled back.

FUN FACT
People who drive lowriders are also called lowriders.

Some lowriders have matching upholstery covering the interior of the car, including the roof.

The last car eased past. Roberto and his dad followed the line of cars. There was a party at the end of the parade. A DJ played loud music. People danced. But the lowriders were the main attraction. Roberto admired the shiny paint and polished wheels. One car was balanced on three wheels! Roberto couldn't believe that was possible.

Cool balancing acts are common ways to demonstrate a lowrider's modifications.

Roberto's dad promised they would fix up a car together. Roberto couldn't wait. His dad had a lowrider when those cars were illegal. They are now legal. But his dad sold his lowrider. They'd have to find a new car to fix. Roberto was excited. Maybe he'd drive in the parade someday.

FUN FACT

People first tried to lower their cars by weighing them down with sandbags.

CHAPTER 2

A Sense of Identity

The Chevrolet Impala sits on cinder blocks. Grass pokes up around the sides. The car is bright blue. Some people paint decorations on their lowriders. Their cars are like works of art. But Maria's dad keeps his simple.

The sun is hot on Maria's neck. She sits in the grass next to her dad. Her mom hums through the open window. Maria sits next to a tool box. Her dad holds out his hand. "Wrench," he says. And Maria hands it to him.

Interesting paint jobs and decals help lowriders stand out.

ZOOM IN ON A
LOWRIDER

Custom steering wheel

Custom upholstery

Fender skirt

Custom paint

Chrome rims

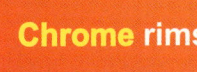

Maria's dad loves his lowrider. He takes Maria cruising in it. Maria helps him fix it. It's a fun way to spend time with her dad. She sticks a rag in her back pocket just like he does. Her fingers are always smudged with grease. Maria's mom clucks at her about it. But Maria knows her mom isn't actually upset. She smiles the whole time.

Maria's parents met because of her dad's lowrider. Her dad tried to impress her mom with his car. Her mom thought it was corny. But she liked cruising in the lowrider. Maria and her family are Mexican American. Lowriding is part of her family's **culture**. Maria's grandparents were lowriders, too. Her great-grandparents were young adults in the 1930s. They were two of the first people in their Los Angeles **barrio** to lower their cars.

HORSE POWER TO HORSEPOWER

Engine power is measured in horsepower. Horsepower is a unit of measurement. It's based on the amount of work a horse could do. Some Mexican men used to show off their horses to women they wanted to impress. Soon, cars became available. Mexican American men didn't show off on horses anymore. Instead, they cruised in cars.

Mexican American history and traditions are still a big part of lowriding culture.

Strict laws against lowriders led to many drivers getting tickets.

Maria is proud of her family's history. Her dad reminds her that lowriders used to be illegal. Cities all over the southwest United States made laws. People couldn't drive cars that were lowered over the tires. Police thought that only criminals drove lowriders. They gave tickets to people who drove lowriders. But they were wrong. The cars are about showing off the driver's identity.

Maria's dad used to raise up his lowrider when he wasn't cruising. But he would still get tickets. It seemed like the laws weren't about the cars. He thought they had more to do with the driver's skin color.

There are still some laws against lowriders. But most of them have changed. Maria and her parents don't have to worry about getting tickets. They cruise together on the weekends. She's glad she can be a part of lowrider culture.

CHAPTER 3

Cruisin'

The car cruises slow and easy down the street. Music streams through the car's custom speakers. Andre flips a switch. The car's **hydraulic** lift system engages.

FUN FACT
There are also lowrider bicycles.

Fluid fills a container under the car. The fluid shoots into an **actuator**. The actuator expands. This causes the lifts to raise. The lowrider seems to hop down the street.

Hydraulic lift systems allow a lowrider's frame and wheels to move up and down.

LOWRIDER
STATS

MODEL	ENGINE SIZE
1964 Chevrolet Impala	8-cylinder
TRANSMISSION	**LIFT SYSTEM**
Automatic	Pro Hopper hydraulic pumps
WHEELS	**SPECIAL FEATURES**
7 inches (18 cm) wide, 13 inches (33 cm) in diameter, gold-painted spokes	Pioneer stereo, green dashboard and steering wheel

Sometimes the lift system moves the car up so its wheels come off the ground. Then it really is hopping. It looks like it's dancing. Andre watched music videos when he was younger. Some of them featured lowriders. The musicians were black, just like Andre. Andre grew up in a neighborhood with lowriders passing through. The drivers took good care of their cars. Andre was excited when he first saw one in a music video. That was when he knew he wanted his own lowrider.

Lowriders are often used in rap and hip-hop music videos.

The music stops. Andre flips the switch. His car lowers back toward the ground. The car has come a long way. It didn't always look like this.

He got this Cadillac Coupe de Ville five years ago. It was a dirty brown color. And it wasn't a lowrider yet.

But Andre was determined. He sanded off all the paint. He added the lift system. He lowered the **chassis**. The fenders covered part of the rear wheels. Then he painted it. He chose emerald green. The paint is flecked with gold. He drives it down the road in the sunlight. There isn't a shinier car around.

The Cadillac Coupe de Ville is a popular lowrider model.

CHAPTER 4

Center of Attention

The stadium's lights shine down over lines of cars. Their different paint colors make a rainbow. Music blares out of speakers. An announcer comes over the air. He invites everyone to the center of the stadium.

Louisa follows her dad through the crowd. She passes rows of shiny cars. She sees a pink Lincoln Continental. It looks like her grandmother's car.

FUN FACT
One of the most famous lowriders is Jesse Valadez's "Gypsy Rose."

Louisa used to go to lowrider shows with her grandma. Louisa's grandma died a couple years ago. Now her dad takes her instead.

One car at the show is two-toned. The top is cream. The bottom is dark red. A chrome bar separates the two colors. Grandma's car was all lavender. She fixed it up herself. Louisa's grandma was one of the first female mechanics in town. She was also one of the best. Some of the men thought she didn't belong. But Louisa's grandma proved them wrong.

Some two-toned lowriders have different colors on the upper and lower halves of the car.

Louisa spent summers with her grandma. She helped fix the car. Louisa's dad didn't have his own lowrider. But they have Grandma's now. Louisa takes care of it. Her dad helps her with some things. But she knows how to fix it and make updates. She'll be able to drive it once she gets her license.

Louisa and her dad reach the stage. They find a good place to watch. There are two cars onstage. They both have special lift systems. Their owners show them off from outside the cars. They use remote controls. Instead of one switch, there are several. One of the cars rises up so it's almost vertical. Its hood points toward the ceiling. The crowd cheers. The other car balances on three wheels. Louisa and her dad clap. The cars come back to the ground. They bang loudly. But they have good springs. They absorb the shock.

Louisa loves going to car shows. She's glad her dad takes her. It's a good way to remember her grandma. And she gets ideas for future projects.

FUN FACT
Lift systems were first used in 1959.

Lift systems can move lowriders into impressive positions.

HOW BIG IS A LOWRIDER?

Height
54 inches
(137 cm)

Variable ground clearance

Length
211 inches (536 cm)

Height
58 inches
(147 cm)

Ground Clearance
6.1 inches
(15.5 cm)

Length
191 inches (485 cm)

LOWRIDER

Width 80 inches (203 cm)

SEDAN

Width 72 inches (183 cm)

BEYOND
THE BOOK

After reading the book, it's time to think about what you learned. Try the following exercises to jumpstart your ideas.

THINK

DIFFERENT SOURCES. Think about the sources you might be able to find about lowriders. What could you learn at a car show? What information would be in an encyclopedia? How could each kind of source be useful in its own way?

CREATE

PRIMARY SOURCES. Primary sources have first-hand information about an event or a period of time. Primary sources can be letters, photographs, or interviews. Create a list of the kinds of primary sources you might be able to find about lowriders.

SHARE

WHAT'S YOUR OPINION?. Lawmakers made lowriders illegal because they thought only criminals drove lowriders. Do you agree or disagree with this decision? Find evidence in the text that supports your position. Share your evidence with a friend. Does your friend find the argument convincing?

GROW

DRAWING CONNECTIONS. Create a diagram to explain the connections between cars and cultural identity. How does learning about different cultures help you understand lowriders?

RESEARCH NINJA

Visit www.ninjaresearcher.com/0585 to learn how to take your research skills and book report writing to the next level!

RESEARCH

DIGITAL LITERACY TOOLS

SEARCH LIKE A PRO
Learn about how to use search engines to find useful websites.

FACT OR FAKE?
Discover how you can tell a trusted website from an untrustworthy resource.

TEXT DETECTIVE
Explore how to zero in on the information you need most.

SHOW YOUR WORK
Research responsibly—learn how to cite sources.

WRITE

GET TO THE POINT
Learn how to express your main ideas.

PLAN OF ATTACK
Learn prewriting exercises and create an outline.

DOWNLOADABLE REPORT FORMS

Further Resources

BOOKS

Adamson, Thomas K. *Lowriders*. Bellwether Media, 2019.

Doeden, Matt. *Lowriders*. Capstone, 2019.

Watts, Pam. *Gasoline Engines*. Focus Readers, 2017.

WEBSITES

FACTSURFER

Factsurfer.com gives you a safe, fun way to find more information.

1. Go to www.factsurfer.com.

2. Enter "Lowriders" into the search box and click 🔍.

3. Select your book cover to see a list of related websites.

Glossary

actuator: An actuator is a device that causes the lift system to engage. Fluid fills the actuator and causes the lift system to raise or lower.

barrio: A barrio is a Mexican American neighborhood. Lowriders started in barrios in the southwestern United States.

chassis: The chassis of the car is the frame that supports it. A lowrider has a chassis that sits low to the ground.

chrome: Chrome is a shiny, silver-colored metal. Many lowriders have chrome accents on the wheels.

culture: Culture is the shared practices of a group of people, such as language, beliefs, music, customs, and more. Maria liked learning about lowriders and their importance in Mexican American culture.

fender: A fender is a piece on a car that covers and protects a wheel. Maria's dad put a fender skirt onto the right rear fender, covering almost the whole wheel.

hydraulic: Hydraulic systems operate using a liquid like oil or water. Lowriders often have hydraulic lift systems.

modifications: Modifications are changes. People took old cars and made modifications to them to create lowriders.

upholstery: Upholstery is the fabric that covers something, especially seating. Some lowriders have velvet upholstery.

Index

actuators, 17

barrios, 12

Cadillac Coupe de Ville, 20

chassis, 21

Chevrolet Impala, 10, 18

culture, 12, 15

fender, 11, 21

horsepower, 13

lift system, 16–17, 18, 19, 21, 24

Lincoln Continental, 22

modifications, 5

music videos, 19

parades, 4, 8

upholstery, 6, 11

wheels, 8, 18, 19, 21, 24

PHOTO CREDITS

The images in this book are reproduced through the courtesy of: Zhao jian kang/Shutterstock Images, front cover (background); Faded Beauty/Shutterstock Images, front cover (car); Roman Belogorodov/Shutterstock Images, p. 3; Roberto Galan/Shutterstock Images, pp. 4–5, 12–13; Bill Chizek/iStockphoto, p. 6; Lissandra Melo/Shutterstock Images, pp. 6–7; Suzanne Tucker/Shutterstock Images, pp. 8–9; Dougberry/iStockphoto, p. 10; laurenbergstrom/iStockphoto, p. 11 (top); Toshifumi Hotchi/Shutterstock Images, pp. 11 (bottom), 14–15, 16–17; Steve Lagreca/Shutterstock Images, p. 18; Joshua Resnick/Shutterstock Images, p. 19; travelfoto/Shutterstock Images, pp. 20–21; Ric Francis/AP Images, p. 22; kenmo/iStockphoto, pp. 22–23; David Tran Photo/Shutterstock Images, pp. 24–25; baileystock/iStockphoto, pp. 26–27 (top); Foto by M/Shutterstock Images, pp. 26–27 (bottom); betto rodrigues/Shutterstock Images, p. 30.

ABOUT THE AUTHOR

Martha London lives in Saint Paul, Minnesota. She writes children's books full-time. When she isn't writing, you can find her hiking in the woods.